Special thanks to Eve Jay, Annelie Wagner, and
Charlie Olsen for their continual help and support

Script by Haiko Hörnig
Art by Marius Pawlitza

First American edition published in 2020 by Graphic Universe™

Graphic Universe™
An imprint of Lerner Publishing Group, Inc.
241 First Avenue North
Minneapolis, MN 55401 USA

For reading levels and more information, look up this title at
www.lernerbooks.com.

Main body text set in CC Dave Gibbons Lower.
Typeface provided by Comicraft.

Library of Congress Cataloging-in-Publication Data

Names: Hörnig, Haiko, 1984– author. | Pawlitza, Marius, 1984– illustrator.
Title: The accursed inheritance of Henrietta Achilles / Haiko Hörnig, Marius Pawlitza.
Other titles: Ein gefährliches Erbe. English
Description: First American edition. | Minneapolis, MN : Graphic Universe, 2020. | Series: A house
    divided ; Book 1 | Audience: Ages 12–18 | Audience: Grades 10–12 | Summary: "After years as an
    orphan, Henrietta Achilles is summoned to the town of Malrenard. She learns she's the only living
    relative of a notorious wizard—and she's just inherited his house and everything in it." —Provided
    by publisher.
Identifiers: LCCN 2019029606 (print) | LCCN 2019029607 (ebook) | ISBN 9781541572430 (library binding)
    | ISBN 9781541586925 (paperback) | ISBN 9781541582330 (ebook)
Subjects: LCSH: Graphic novels. | CYAC: Graphic novels. | Inheritance and succession—Fiction. |
    Blessing and cursing—Fiction. | Magic—Fiction.
Classification: LCC PZ7.7.H665 Ac 2020 (print) | LCC PZ7.7.H665 (ebook) | DDC 741.5/973—dc23

LC record available at https://lccn.loc.gov/2019029606
LC ebook record available at https://lccn.loc.gov/2019029607

Manufactured in the United States of America
1-46520-47549-8/28/2019

A HOUSE DIVIDED

THE ACCURSED INHERITANCE OF HENRIETTA ACHILLES

HAIKO HÖRNIG • MARIUS PAWLITZA

GRAPHIC UNIVERSE™ • MINNEAPOLIS

BOOM

GET DOWN!

SOUNDS LIKE WE'LL HAVE TO WAIT FOR THAT RAINBOW A BIT LONGER...

YOU STAY *HERE* I'LL LOOK FOR YOUR FATHER.

NO! DON'T LEAVE ME, MOM!

WHATEVER HAPPENS, YOU *DON'T* OPEN THIS DOOR. UNDERSTOOD?

KLUNG

BOOM

MOM? ARE YOU *OKAY?*

C'MON, OPEN!

OPEN UP!

KLACK

BANG

BANG

BANG

BANG

BANG

DON'T.

DON'T LEAVE ME...

HUH?

IT'S *RENAULT!*

RENAULT IS *BACK!*

AH, *RENAULT!* DEAR OLD RENAULT! HOW GOOD TO HAVE YOU BACK! HOW *ARE* YOU?

YOUR JOURNEY WAS A *SUCCESS,* I PRESUME?

INDEED, MAYOR BRASSINGTON. AS I WROTE IN MY *LETTER,* I...

YES, YES, NOW LET'S HAVE A LOOK AT...

...OUR MOST WELCOME *VISITORS!*

COUGH

COUGH

MR. MAYOR, MAY I INTRODUCE...

...MISS *HENRIETTA ACHILLES.*

HEH...HEH HEH... WHERE ARE THE PARENTS?

I'M AFRAID MISS ACHILLES IS OUR **ONLY** GUEST.

ARE YOU OUT OF YOUR MIND, RENAULT?

WELL, MR. MAYOR, ACCORDING TO OUR DOCUMENTS, SHE IS THE **LAST** LIVING RELATIVE! WHAT WAS I SUPPOSED TO DO?

JUST TELL ME THIS: HOW IS A **LITTLE GIRL** GOING TO SOLVE OUR **PROBLEM**?

DO YOU HAVE TO **FIGHT** IN FRONT OF THE CHILD? POOR THING JUST LOST HER **UNCLE!**

BUMP

I'M **EDNA ALBINSON.** WELCOME TO MALRENARD...

I'M SORRY FOR YOUR LOSS. YOU MUST BE DEVAST--

WELL, THERE'S NO HELPING IT! BETTER GET ON WITH THE LEGAL STUFF! NO TIME TO WASTE!

SLAP!

FOR GOD'S SAKE, RORRIN. LET HER CATCH HER BREATH FIRST.

YOU HUNGRY, CHILD? THIRSTY?

ACTUALLY, I'M QUITE ALL RI--

LET'S GET SOMETHING WARM IN THAT FRAIL FRAME OF YOURS. THERE'LL STILL BE TIME FOR *MOURNING* AFTER A STEAMING BOWL OF SOUP!

FIRST THINGS FIRST!

ALL RIGHT THEN! BEAT IT, YOU LOT! GIVE OUR NEW ARRIVAL SOME *SPACE*, WILL YA?

DRIP!

TAP

TAP

TAP

AH, YES, YOU'RE PROBABLY WONDERING ABOUT THE ENORMOUS FENCE AROUND THE *GRAVEYARD*...

I REALLY WASN'T.

AND THE COMPLETELY *REASONABLE* ANSWER IS TO FEND OFF THE FOXES, OF COURSE! HEH HEH HEH. HEH.

KRA- KOOOMM

SPEAR TIPS BENDING *INWARD* TO KEEP FOXES AWAY. COMPLETELY REASONABLE. RIGHT.

WILD MUG

BAAAH!

TONIGHT, YOU'LL STAY AT *MY* PLACE, DEAR.

DID YOU KNOW MY UNCLE, MA'AM?

WELL...NOT *PERSONALLY.* BUT HE WAS QUITE FAMOUS AROUND HERE. ESPECIALLY FOR HIS EXPLOITS IN THE *WAR,* OF COURSE.

PEOPLE TOLD STORIES ABOUT HIM EVEN *BEFORE* HE CAME TO MALRENARD.

EVERYBODY KNEW OF THE GREAT *ORNUN ZOL.*

NOT ME.

SO, YOU WANNA KNOW ABOUT ORNUN ZOOOOL, HUH?

LEMME TELL YOU ABOUT ORNUN ZOOOOOOOL...

HE WUZ A NO-GOOD WIZZAD! YES HE WUZ!

SKRASH

AN' I DON' GIVE A RAT'S BEHIND IF THAT BLASTED *HOUSE* OF HIS...

...IS FILLED WITH TREAS--

SO SORRY, AGAIN!

COOCKARACOOOO

BAAAH!

LOOK ON THE **BRIGHT** SIDE, KID. YOUR UNCLE WAS A WEALTHY MAN.

ALTHOUGH THE TWO OF YOU NEVER MET, HE LEFT YOU A QUITE **SIZABLE** ESTATE...

...AS WELL AS A, HEH, CONSIDERABLE FORTUNE. WHICH IS LIKELY HIDDEN ALL OVER THE HOUSE.

HERE YOU'LL FIND THE BELONGINGS THAT WERE FOUND AT THE SITE.

AT THE **SITE?**

WHERE HIS BODY **EVAPORATED.**

LIGHTNING STRIKE. A FREAK ACCIDENT, BY THE LOOKS OF IT.

AND THESE ARE... HNNG...THE **KEYS** TO THE MANOR, OF COURSE.

SIGN **HERE.**

AND **HERE.**

AND WITH **THIS,** YOU'RE NOW THE OWNER OF THE ESTATE!

AND FULLY ACCOUNTABLE FOR EVERYTHING THAT HAPPENS TO THE HOUSE...

...OR IS **CAUSED** BY IT.

IT'S NOT TRUE, YOU KNOW.

THE DEAD GUY? ORNUN ZOL? HE'S *NOT* MY UNCLE.

I'VE NEVER EVEN *HEARD* OF HIM, AND NOW THAT HE'S DEAD, *MY* NAME POPS UP IN SOME RANDOM DOCUMENTS?

"A POOR ORPHAN GIRL JUST HAPPENS TO INHERIT THE FABULOUS WEALTH OF HER MYSTERIOUS UNCLE..."

PFFF! YEAH, RIGHT! GIVE ME A BREAK! PRETTY SURE I'VE READ *THAT* STORY IN ONE OR TWO OF MY BOOKS.

I MEAN, IF HE REALLY *WAS* MY UNCLE, HE WOULD'VE TRIED TO CONTACT ME. RIGHT? HE WOULDN'T HAVE JUST LEFT ME IN THAT...PLACE.

AND HERE WE ARE! YOUR *STOP*.

OFF YOU GO. HAVE FUN WITH YOUR MANSION.

OH, AND DON'T MIND THE WAR.

UMM, ARE WE TALKING ABOUT THE WAR THAT ENDED *NINE YEARS* AGO? BECAUSE I'M PRETTY SURE THAT WON'T BE A PROBLEM...

NAH, NOT THE OLD *GRAND WAR*...

I MEAN THE ONE INSIDE YOUR *HOUSE*.

UH, WHAT?

WHAₐₐₐₐAₐ...

SO WHICH ONE OF YOU IS IT?

LOOKS ABOUT RIGHT.

COME ON! FIT, YOU STUPID KEY!

HNNG!

THUD

WAIT A MINUTE! THE KEYHOLE'S JUST PAINTED--

--ON!

SNAP!

WAAAAAH!

SHIIIIINNG!

FFFZ ZZZ ZH!

WHOA!

CLICK
CLUNK

CREEEEAAAAK

27

WOOSH

SQUEEEEEAK

HALT IN THE NAME OF THE MARGRAVE! LAY DOWN THE STOLEN PROVISIONS AND SURRENDER!

OUTTA THE WAY! STOLEN PROVISIONS COMING THROUGH!

HOT!

HOT!

HOT!

WELL, NOW YOU'VE MADE ME *REALLY* ANGRY!

NOT AS ANGRY AS CAPTAIN BOONER WILL BE WHEN HE HEARS ABOUT HOW YOU LET THEM INTO THE PANTRY!

THEY *KNOCKED!* WHO EVER HEARD OF BURGLARS KNOCKING?

HM.

LET'S GIVE 'EM HELL, BOSS!

I'M KINDA--OOH!...

...IN THE MIDDLE OF SOMETHING HERE.

HAHAHA! GO ON AND CRY, YOU BIG BABIES! WE SHALL DRINK YOUR TEARS WHILE WE FEAST ON YOUR FOOD!

YOU'RE HUNGRY? THEN *EAT SPEAR!*

OKAY, I'LL SHUT UP NOW!

YAY.

31

WHOMPH!

FLUMP

RUMBLE

RUMBLE

FWOP

TAP

HUH!

NAAAAAAAAAH!

BUMP

COULD WE PLEASE **STOP** ADDING TO THE LOAD?

TAK

TAK

TAK

IS SHE READY, ROOSTER?

YES... GASP... SIR! COMING RIGHT... UP!

FASTER, LAD!

WHOAREYOU WHATISTHIS IDON'TEVEN--

WE ARE...

FIRE!

...IN A BIT OF A PICKLE.

BOOM!

JUMP!

BAHM

AH! *MUCH* BETTER!

YOU OKAY, BOSS?

OUCH. I'M JUST SPLENDID.

ON YOUR FEET! RETREAT MANEUVER *"DANCING BASILISK!"*

WHICH ONE IS THAT AGAIN?

THE ONE WHERE WE *SPLIT UP* AND MEET BACK AT CAMP! WHY DO I EVEN BOTHER COMING UP WITH *AWESOME* STRATEGY NAMES IF NONE OF YOU BOTHER TO LEARN THEM?

THIS IS CRAZY! WHO *ARE* YOU GUYS AND WHAT'S *HAPPENING* AND WHY IS EVERYTHING *EXPLODING?*

WELL, IT'S KIND OF COMPLICATED...

TAP

TAP

TAP

TAP

TAP

KLUNK!

NATE FLEMMING, ALSO KNOWN AS THE KNIGHT OF KNAVES...

OKAY, SO MAYBE IT'S NOT THAT COMPLICATED AFTER ALL.

HUFF

HUFF

...YOU ARE UNDER ARREST FOR *THIEVERY* AND *CRIMES* AGAINST THE MARGRAVE!

TIME TO BAIL, KID! *NOW!*

I'M *NOT...* GOING TO LET HIM...DIE!

BA NG!

DOWN!

WHIZZ ZZ Z

WHUMP!

GOTCHA, BIG GUY!

HE'S *FINE.* LET'S GET OUTTA HERE!

TAP TAP TAP

MISSED HIM, SIR.

DON'T WORRY, RODRIGUEZ.

WE'LL GET HIM *EVENTUALLY*.

YOU'RE A *RUNAWAY*, HUH?

TOUGH LUCK THEN.

NOW HOW DO I GET OUT OF HERE?

WHAT'S IN THIS VAULT?

YOU'RE PROBABLY TOO YOUNG TO REMEMBER THE LAST DAYS OF THE GRAND WAR...

NO, I'M *NOT!*

OH-KAAAY...

PUFF

PUFF

IN THE LAST DAYS OF THE WAR, THINGS LOOKED BAD FOR US.

WELL THEN.

I MEAN *REALLY* BAD.

THE ENEMY HAD INVADED MUCH OF OUR LAND...

...AND THEIR BOMBERS RAINED DOWN FIERY DEATH...

...ON EVERYONE DARING TO RESIST.

THEN ONE DAY CAME WORD OF A MAN WHO HAD FOUND A WAY.

WHO WIELDED A MYSTICAL POWER THAT COULD TURN THE TIDES.

THAT MAN WAS *ORNUN ZOL!*

BACK THEN, OF COURSE, WE DIDN'T BELIEVE A WORD. NOTHING MORE THAN A SILLY FAIRY TALE.

WELL, WE WERE *WRONG.*

ORNUN ZOL USED THIS MYSTICAL POWER--OR *WHATEVER* IT WAS--AND ENDED THE GRAND WAR IN A SINGLE NIGHT.

FFFP

FFFP

COUGH!

WHEEZE!

BARF!

GOOD GRIEF! THIS STUFF TASTES LIKE MUMMIFIED MERMAID! THE *TAIL* PART!

DID YOU... SEE IT?

THE END OF THE WAR?

ME?

NAAAH.

ANYWAY, THE STORY GOES THAT HE SEALED HIS POWER IN A *VAULT* HIDDEN SOMEWHERE IN THIS HOUSE.

WHEN NEWS OF HIS DEATH TRAVELED THROUGH THE COUNTRY...

...I FIGURED *SOMEBODY* SHOULD GO LOOKING FOR THIS INCREDIBLY VALUABLE THING!

YOU KNOW, FOR *SAFEKEEPING!*

BACK TO GETTING OUT OF HERE...

MY GUYS ARE PROBABLY WAITING AT OUR CAMP IN THE CONSERVATORY, SO THAT'S WHERE I WANT TO GO.

K RR

THE HOUSE HAS A CONSERVATORY?

WELL, THAT'S WHAT IT WAS BEFORE GRETCHEN ACCIDENTALLY TURNED ON THE SPRINKLERS. NOW IT'S MORE LIKE AN INDOOR JUNGLE.

A LONG UNCERTAIN ROAD AHEAD OF HER, SHE DARED NOT SET ONE FOOT IN FRONT OF THE OTHER.

OH, COME ON! DON'T BE COY! WHICH OF THESE HALLWAYS LEADS TO THE CONSERVATORY?

WHEN SHE LOOKED OVER HER SHOULDER, THE WAY BEHIND HER...

...WAS EVEN LESS WELCOMING.

WHAT'S THAT SUPPOSED TO MEAN? I REALLY DON'T HAVE THE TIME FOR *SILLY RIDDLES!*

? ?

I *KNOW* THIS ONE!

I KNOW WHAT HE *MEANS!*

WHAT THE...

48

IT'S **NOT** A RIDDLE!

WHIZZZ

N...O...P...

AHA!

...Q...R...S...

IT'S A **QUOTE!**

TA-DAA!

WOW! THE FOURTH VOLUME!

The Adventures of Virginia Sly IV

I'VE BEEN LOOKING FOR THIS ONE FOR YEARS!

MY MOM USED TO READ IT TO ME.

LEMME SEE! MAYBE THERE'S A CLUE INSIDE!

HMM. THE *FIRST* ONE IS MISSING.

CLICK

KRRR

RR

NOT SURE WHAT I DID THERE, BUT I THINK SOMETHING'S HAPPENI--

iiiiiiijjiiii...

...iiiiiiiiiiiiii...

KRR

KRRR

...ING!

WUP

WUP

WUP

ENJOYING THE VIEW?

PLEASE, TAKE YOUR... HNNG... TIME!

WELL, NOW! A SECRET STAIRWAY ON THE OUTSIDE? STRANGE... BUT ENTICING.

GOTTA HAND IT TO YOU, KID. YOU'RE FULL OF SURPRISES!

YOU MIGHT EVEN *SURVIVE* THIS MADNESS.

YOU COMING?

WE'VE GOT MUSCLE, BUT WE CAN ALWAYS USE ANOTHER BRAIN.

THANKS, BUT... I DON'T THINK I'M A BANDIT. SORRY.

RIGHT. MY MISTAKE.

HEY!

YOUR SHARE OF THE SPOILS.

WHOP

THERE'S MORE WHERE THAT CAME FROM, WHEN YOU DECIDE WHO YOU *ARE*.

MUNCH

GRRRRRR

GULP

OKAAAY. I'M JUST GONNA HEAD STRAIGHT TO THE FOYER, PICK UP MY THINGS, AN...

STRAIGHT TO THE FOYER.

AS YOU WISH.

WAAAA!

THEY WILL RUE THE DAY THEY STOLE MY PERFECT *PASTRY!*

HEY, I FOUND SOME STUFF.

NO SIGN OF THE BANDITS. THEY MUST HAVE SCURRIED BACK INTO THEIR SLIMEY HIDEY-HOLES!

I'M GONNA *GET* THEM FASTER THAN YOU CAN SAY "QUICHE-STEALING BANDIT SCU--"

KRRR

AAAAAAAH!

WHUMP!

WOW. HE'S GOOD.

GOOD NEWS, CAPTAIN! CAUGHT US ONE OF FLEMMING'S SCOUNDRELS.

HM. I KNEW FLEMMING WAS A DEPRAVED INDIVIDUAL...

...BUT I DIDN'T KNOW HE WAS RECRUITING CHILDREN.

MMHPF!

HE DITCHED YOU TO SAVE HIMSELF, HM?

THAT'S NOT TRUE, HE--

YOUR BOY FLEMMING IS A *WANTED* CRIMINAL!

DON'T BE FOOLED BY HIS *WARM* SMILE OR HIS *GOLDEN* LOCKS!

OR BY THE *CUTE* DIMPLES IN HIS ROSY CHEEKS...

ESPECIALLY NOT THOSE!

THEY ARE KNOWN TO KILL!

LISTEN, I'M *NOT* A BANDIT! YOU HAVE TO BELIEVE ME!

SO WHAT *ARE* YOU THEN?

WELL, UH, I'M...

...THE OWNER. OF THE HOUSE.

I GUESS.

WHICH **MEANS**... YOU ARE...

YOU ARE ALL TRESPASSERS.

THAT'S **RIGHT!** SO YOU BETTER GET OUT OF **MY** HOUSE. RIGHT **NOW!**

HA HA HA HA HA!

SORRY, GIRL. YOU JUST DON'T LOOK LIKE MUCH OF A WIZARD TO ME.

AND I CAN **SMELL** A LIAR!

THEY SMELL LIKE...

SNNNIIIIIFFF

...QUIIIIIIIICHE!

JUST TELL ME ONE THING, THIEF!

WAS IT **DELICIOUS?**

OKAY, I ADMIT I TOOK A BITE. BUT YOU GUYS TOOK A **SHOT** AT ME!

WE'LL LEAVE AS SOON AS WE'VE PUT FLEMMING AND HIS BAND OF ROGUES IN IRONS. ORDERS OF THE MARGRAVE.

JUST TELL US WHERE YOUR FRIENDS ARE, AND WE'LL LET YOU GO.

Conservatory

MAYBE WE SHOULD TAKE A LOOK AT THE CONSERVATORY...

OH! UH...

...HERE I WAS THINKING...

...YOU WERE LOOKING FOR THE *SECRET VAULT.*

MAYBE THERE'S MORE TO YOU THAN MEETS THE EYE.

WHAM

SIR! SIR!

WE ARE UNDER ATTACK!

FLEMMING IS BACK ALREADY?

NO, SIR. IT'S THOSE *KOBOLDS* AGAIN!

HA! THOSE LITTLE PESTS ARE PROBABLY STILL MAD WE SET UP CAMP IN THEIR OLD LAIR.

I'LL SHOO 'EM AWAY!

CRASH

WAAARGH!!

NO TIME TO PANIC... LET'S GO!

STAY CALM.

STAY CALM.

DON'T FREAK OUT!

NEXT STOP: MASTER BEDROOM.

HUH?

WOOSH

WOOOAAH...

SSSSSSST

AAAAAH!!

CLICK

WOOAH!!

UFF!

SSSST!

SSSST

OOF

REMIND ME TO NEVER FACE MY FEARS AGAIN. UGH.

WHEEZE

SO THIS MUST BE IT. THE BEDROOM...

...OF ORNUN ZOL.

WHY ME?

THIS HOUSE... THIS LIFE...

NO ONE ASKED IF I WANTED ANY OF THIS.

RUSTLE

WAIT A MINUTE, IS THAT A...?

NO WAY!

COME ON.
COME ON.
COME ON.

CRUUUNK

CRUUUNK

CRUUUNK
RUMBLE

PSHHH

YES! HOT WATER, EVEN!

TEARS OF THE KRAKEN

NO. I *KNOW* IT.

I THINK I CAN DO THIS.

WHATEVER "THIS" IS.

SO THESE ARE THE THINGS HE HAD WITH HIM WHEN HE DIED.

HM. A CANDLE.

SOME DICE.

A STRANGE COIN.

AND THE KEYS, OF COURSE.

NO IDEA WHAT THIS ALL MEANS. HOPE YOU DIDN'T BET ON ME TO SOLVE YOUR MURDER, UNCLE.

YAWN

WELL, MAYBE I'LL GET IT TOMORROW.

SO SOFT AND **COMFY.**

MAYBE THIS WON'T BE SO BAD AFTER ALL.

PFFF

HENRIETTAAAA.

I KNOW YOU ARE HERE.

WOOOOSH

TSHING

I **SMELLED** YOU THE MOMENT YOU STEPPED OUT OF THE CARRIAGE.

OOF

I... I DON'T UNDERSTAND. I DON'T KNOW YOU.

THEN LET ME HELP YOU REMEMBER!

PLEASE, I DON'T...

B**OO**M

B**OO**M

B**OO**M

NO... THIS CAN'T BE REAL...

I'M BACK IN THE *BUNKER!*

HEEEEELP! SOMEBODY OPEN THE DOOR!

COME ON! OPEN! PLEASE!

PLEASE!

HOW...?

OOFF!

YOU KNOW WHAT? I DON'T CARE **HOW!**

I DON'T CARE ABOUT **MELTED** MONSTERS!

I DON'T CARE ABOUT MAGIC, HIDDEN VAULTS, BANDITS, OR QUICHE WARS!

AND I ESPECIALLY DON'T CARE ABOUT THIS STUPID **HOUSE!**

TAP TAP TAP

TWA CK

WHERE ARE YOU...?

RATTLE
RATTLE
FLUSH
KLONG

HM?

WHAT WAS *THAT?*

SOUNDED LIKE SOMETHING *BIG* GOT FLUSHED DOWN THE DRAIN.

WASN'T *ME*, I SWEAR.

I HAVEN'T BEEN TO THE LOO IN DAYS!

TOO MUCH INFORMATION, RUNGO!

HM.

SOUNDS LIKE THAT FLEA-RIDDEN PIRATE'S ALREADY BACK.

BANG BANG BANG

CHANGING OF THE GUARD IS STILL AN HOUR AWAY!

BANG
BANG

BANG

YEAH, YEAH, DON'T BURST A--

BANG
BANG

AW...!

TOLD YOU IT WOULD WORK!

BOOOOOOSS? IT'S FOR YOU!

THE GAME'S OVER, FLEMMING.

DON'T EMBARRASS YOURSELF.

TWITCH

YOU'RE NOT GETTING OUT OF THIS ONE.

WELL, IT'S A PITY THAT--

SCREE@ONKH

HUH? COME AGAIN?

I SAID, IT'S A PITY THAT--

RUUNKH

TAP

TAP

HERE YOU GO.

WHAM

CLANG

WHAT IS THE MEANING OF *THIS*?

I'M GOING BACK TO ST. GENEVIEVE. YOU CAN *KEEP* THE HOUSE.

OR GIVE IT TO SOMEONE ELSE. *I* DON'T CARE.

TAP

TAP

TAP

NOW, WAIT A MINUTE, YOUNG LADY!

REMEMBER, YOU'VE SIGNED A BINDING **CONTRACT!**

JUST LOOK AROUND YOU! CAN'T YOU **SEE** WHAT THAT HOUSE HAS DONE TO THIS COMMUNITY?

MUNCH

TAKE OL' GEORGE HERE! HE USED TO BE OUR **BARBER!**

BAAAA

ONE DAY, HE WALKED TOO CLOSE TO THAT DEVILISH HOUSE, AND **ZAP!** HE'S A SHEEP! NOW EVERYBODY'S CRITICIZING HIS HAIRCUTTING TECHNIQUE!

MESSED UP MY **BANGS** TOO, HE DID!

AND SINCE YESTERDAY, WE'VE ALSO GOT A **GIANT RAT PROBLEM!**

WILD MU

GULP GULP GULP

GIMME BACK MY **HAMMER!**

GIMME BACK MY **CHICKEN!**

SQUEEK!

EVER SINCE THE OLD WIZARD DIED, THIS TOWN HAS BEEN OVERRUN WITH ESCAPING **MONSTERS** AND MISFIRED **CURSES!** ALL COMING FROM THAT INFERNAL **HOUSE!**

86

HNNG...THE CURRENT IS TOO **STRONG!**

GET ON THAT *RAT!* THE KOBOLDS HAVE TRAINED THEM AS *MOUNTS!*

KOBOLDS?

HOW...HOW IS THIS POSSIBLE? WE'VE *NEVER* HAD A FLOOD IN MALRENARD!

MUNCH

THE *HOUSE.* IT'S COMING FROM THE HOUSE.

TO BE CONTINUED...

Swain's Quiche

WHAM!

Hands off or
I cut them
off!!

DOUGH:

- 2 cups plain flour
- ½ teaspoon salt
- 10 tablespoons cold butter
- 3–4 tbsp (50 milliliters) cold water

FILLING:

- 7 oz bacon (4–5 slices thick-cut bacon), cubed
- ½ onion, sliced
- ½ red bell pepper, diced
- 3 tablespoons tomato paste
- 8 ounces (240 ml) heavy whipping cream
- 5 eggs
- 2 cups shredded cheese (half Swiss, half cheddar)
- A pinch of pepper, salt, and nutmeg

ALSO:

- 10-inch (25-centimeter) pie pan
- shortening for the pan
- flour for dusting the counter

Whisk together the flour and salt. Cut the butter into the flour mixture using a fork or pastry blender. Mix in the water with a fork until dough just starts to come together. Knead lightly to form a smooth dough. Pat dough into a circle and refrigerate for 30 minutes.

(You can use this time to make the filling.)

THEN:

Grease baking pan.

Reserve one third of the dough for the lattice crust.

Roll out the remaining dough on a lightly floured surface. Then put dough in the pie pan so it overlaps the edges of the pan by 0.5- to 1-inch (1.3–2.5 cm).

Roll out the reserved dough and cut into ½-inch (1.3 cm) thick ribbons. Set aside.

Preheat the oven to 350°F.

Fry bacon bits until crisp. Sauté onions in a separate pan until soft. Add in diced pepper and sauté together. Mix in tomato paste, then add the bacon. Turn down heat and add half of the cream (½ cup [120 ml]). Stir together, turn off the heat, and let cool.

Whisk eggs in a medium bowl. Mix in remaining ½-cup cream. Stir in salt, pepper, and nutmeg. Add in the onion mixture and fold in the cheese.

Pour the filling evenly into the pan.

Weave the dough ribbons into a lattice pattern on top of the filling. Adhere them to the sides of the crust using a dab of cold water to help the dough stick.

Put quiche in the preheated oven for 45 minutes or until the crust is golden brown and the filling has thickened. To check for doneness, a knife inserted into the middle of the quiche should come out clean.

45 MIN

FINAL STEP:

Let it cool down and serve it either warm or cold.

Bon Appetit!

IN THE NEXT INSTALLMENT OF A HOUSE DIVIDED...

ABOUT THE AUTHOR

Haiko Hörnig spent his childhood in his parents' comic book store, where he developed a love for sequential art at an early age. In middle school, he quickly became friends with Marius Pawlitza. The two of them first enjoyed role-playing games together and later started to make comics. Since 2013, Haiko has worked as a screenwriter for animated shows and feature films. A House Divided is his first published book series. He is based in Frankfurt, Germany. He's also active on Twitter (@DerGrafX) and Instagram (@ahousedividedcomic).

ABOUT THE ILLUSTRATOR

Marius Pawlitza was born in Poland in 1984 and grew up in Ludwigshafen, Germany. Years later, he studied communication design in the German city of Mainz. It was a good excuse to spend as much time as possible playing video games and making comics with Haiko Hörnig. Since 2011, he has worked as an art director for different agencies and companies in Frankfurt, in addition to creating sequential art. On Twitter, he's @pengboom.